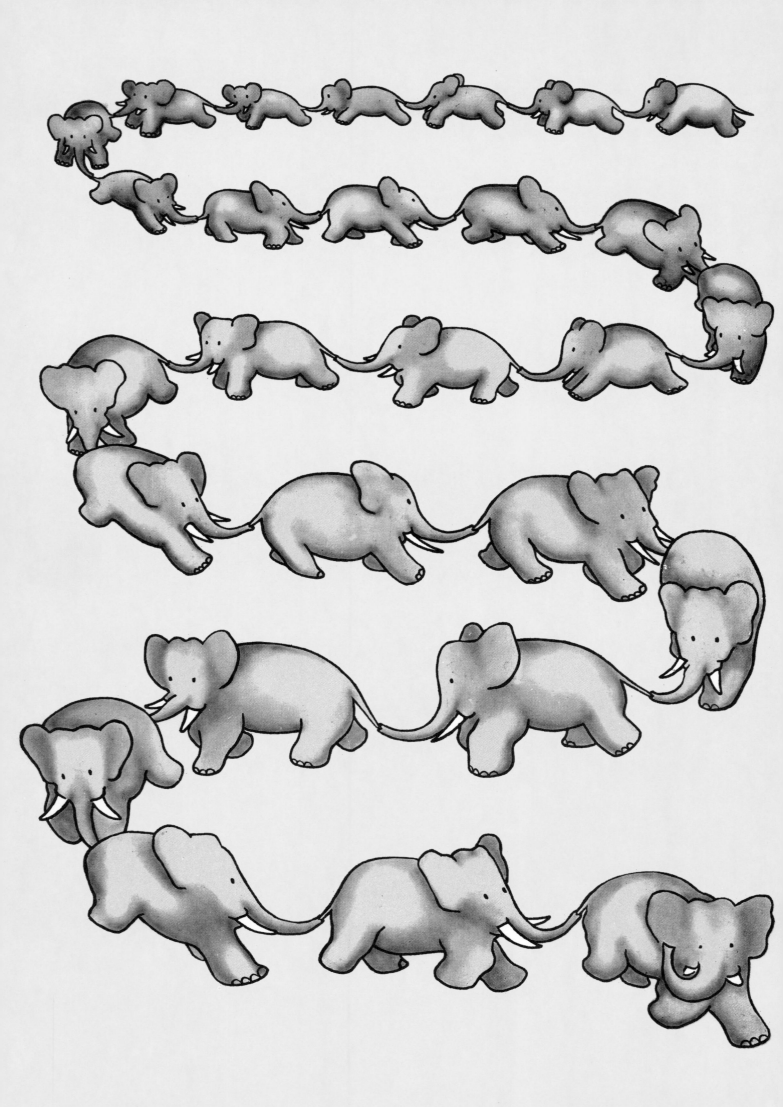

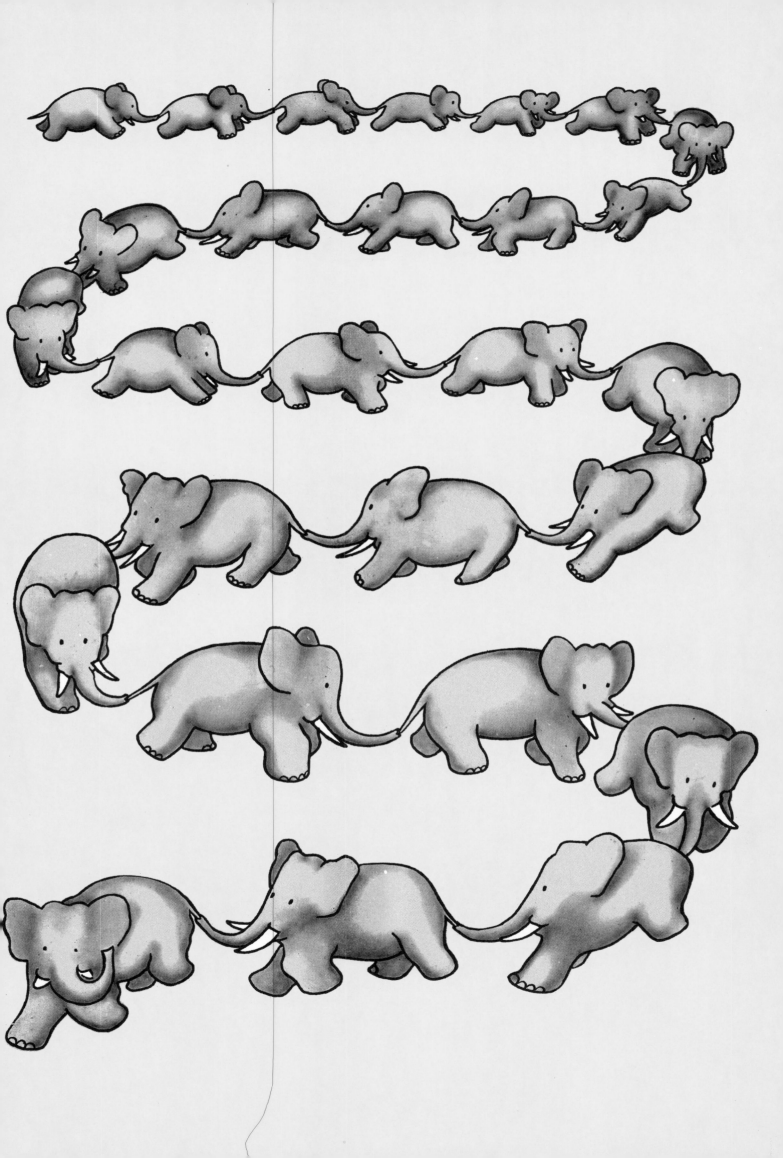

BABAR'S BATTLE

BY LAURENT DE BRUNHOFF

Random House 🏠 New York

Library of Congress Cataloging-in-Publication Data
Brunhoff, Laurent de, 1925– Babar's battle / Laurent de Brunhoff. p. cm. SUMMARY: Discord between the elephants
and the rhinoceroses threatens to lead to war, but King Babar has a plan of his own. ISBN 0-679-81068-4 (trade)—
ISBN 0-679-91068-9 (lib. bdg.) [1. Elephants—Fiction. 2. Rhinoceros—Fiction. 3. War—Fiction.] I. Title.
PZ7.B82843Babit 1992 [E]—dc20 91-53169

Manufactured in the United States of America 10 9 8 7 6 5 4 3 2 1

In Celesteville, the elephants had been living happily for many years. They had been at peace with their neighbors, the rhinoceroses.

One lovely day, when Babar, the king of the elephants, and Celeste, his queen, were out for a walk with their children, Babar happened to think of Rataxes, who ruled the rhinos. "That Rataxes is a bad one," he said, "but he hasn't bothered us for a long time."

"That could change in a second," said Celeste. "Rataxes has caused trouble before, and he could again. I don't trust him."

Celeste was right.

For some time Rataxes had been visiting a witch named Macidexia in her underground cavern. She hated Babar and kept urging Rataxes to get rid of him.

"Babar thinks he's so great," she said one day. "You should invite him to dinner, as though you were friends, and then have him killed."

"Killed? Oh no, not really!" he exclaimed. "But perhaps it would be enough to take him prisoner. Yes, that's a good idea! We'll take him prisoner. I'll invite him immediately."

Babar and Celeste received the invitation for a friendly dinner at Rataxes' palace. As they dressed for the evening, Babar said, "A friendly dinner! You see, he really has gotten nice."

"Perhaps he's acting nice to lower your guard. Be careful," Celeste replied.

And so, with their friend General Cornelius, Babar and Celeste went to have dinner at Rataxes' palace.

The dinner was a great success. The chef prepared a dozen delicious dishes, and the elephants ate to their hearts' delight. Rataxes enjoyed himself so much that he completely forgot

about giving the sign to seize the guests. His soldiers, who were
waiting to jump on the elephants and take them prisoner, waited
in vain for the signal.

Late that night Rataxes saw the elephants to their car.
Everyone felt wonderful after such a glorious feast.

"Next time you'll come have dinner with us in Celesteville!"
said Babar as the car drove off.

Rataxes descended the path to the grotto. He had promised
Macidexia he would come as soon as dinner was over to give her
the details of the ambush.

"What am I going to tell her?" Rataxes asked himself as he
walked farther and farther down to Macidexia's grotto.

"You idiot!" screamed Macidexia. "You had the chance to get rid of Babar forever." She spun around with fury, then stopped and faced him squarely. "But I have another good idea.

Empty the lake at Celesteville! Without water, the elephants will be at our mercy."

And Rataxes, feeling bad about his failure to have Babar seized, passed on the order to empty the lake.

The rhinoceros engineers installed a powerful pump in a hidden spot to **drain** the water out of the lake. Immediately the water **began** flowing into the neighboring valley and out **to** sea. A company of guards stood nearby to keep **an** eye on the pump.

The water level sank rapidly. The creatures who lived in the lake were confused. The flamingos asked the ducks what was happening, the ducks asked the frogs, the frogs asked the fish.

At the palace, when Celeste began to fill the tub for
Isabelle's bath, no water came out of the faucet. Isabelle found
that amusing, but Celeste was worried.

"What will become of us if there's no more water?" she
asked herself.

The gardener was upset too. There was no way to water the flowers. "How dry it is this year!" he said to the children. "The lake has never sunk so low before."

"A dry year?" said Arthur. "I don't believe it. Something funny's going on."

The elephants were in despair to see their once-beautiful lake all dry. There was nothing left but a few puddles. What would they do without water? It was impossible to truck in enough for the whole city.

Babar, Cornelius, and Arthur got together to discuss the situation.

"I bet Rataxes is behind this," said Arthur.

"You may be right," said Babar. "Celeste thinks so too."

Pom, Flora, Alexander, and little Isabelle had fun walking barefoot in the mud.

On one of their walks they discovered the pump, hidden under some branches. They saw that someone was using the pump to drain the lake. Just then a rhino guard came running out of the bushes and shouted, "Get lost!"

The children ran back home to tell Babar what they had seen.

Babar called Rataxes on the phone. "What's wrong
with you?" he said. "Have you gone crazy? I thought we
were friends."

"You think you're so great," said Rataxes. "But my army
will pound yours into the ground."

With a heavy heart, Babar understood that he had to prepare
his army for war.

The next morning at sunrise, Babar went to see the field
of battle. His soldiers had worked hard all night to oil and shine
their armor.

"Cornelius," he said, "I've been thinking. I want to avoid a

war, so I am going to challenge Rataxes to battle it out between the two of us."

"But Babar, what if you're beaten?"

"I know how to fight Rataxes. I'm going to use the sun to win."

Rataxes insisted on having the sun at his back in order to
make it shine in Babar's eyes and put him at a disadvantage.
Babar had known Rataxes would do that, but he had a plan.

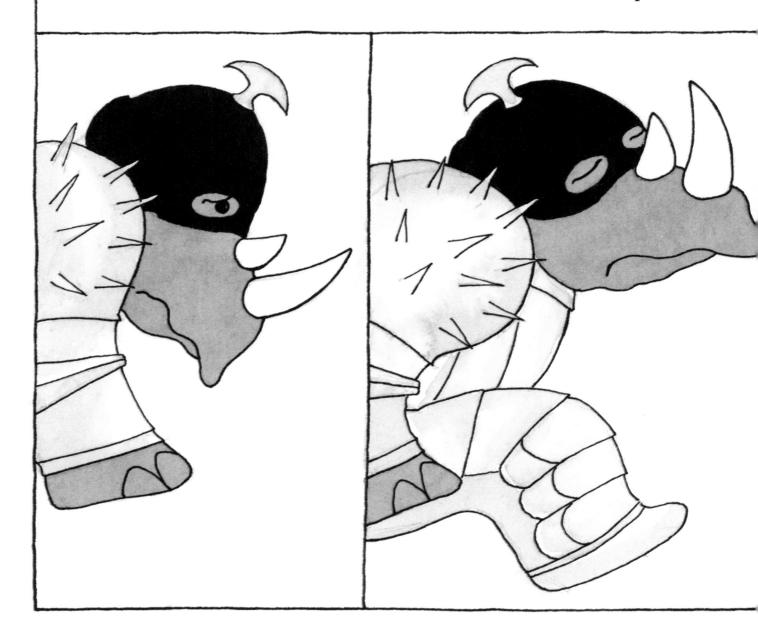

When Rataxes charged, Babar raised his shield and sent the ray of sunlight streaming back into Rataxes' eyes. The rhinoceros kept running toward Babar, even though he couldn't see a thing.

Bam! Blinded by the sun, Rataxes ran into a tree, where his horns got stuck. He thrashed about but couldn't get free. Babar's scheme had worked!

Macidexia saw everything from the rhinoceroses' camp and let out shrieks of rage and despair. Her chance to defeat King Babar was gone forever.

The elephant gardener, using a power saw, cut down the tree to free Rataxes. The unhappy rhinoceros tried to make excuses. He was sorry for what he had done and wished he hadn't listened to Macidexia.

"It isn't my fault!" he said. "Macidexia made me do it!" He agreed to disarm his soldiers and to remove the pump that was draining the lake.

Macidexia returned to her grotto, screaming and stamping her feet. She shook the columns so hard that they cracked. With a thundering roar, the grotto fell in on top of her. The rhino witch was dead!

A few days later some heavy rain fell at last on Celesteville, and the lake filled up, little by little.

How beautiful the lake is now! It seems even more beautiful than before. Everyone wants to go on forever diving, splashing,

and swimming in the cold and clear water. The mothers don't even mind that the children have stayed in too long.

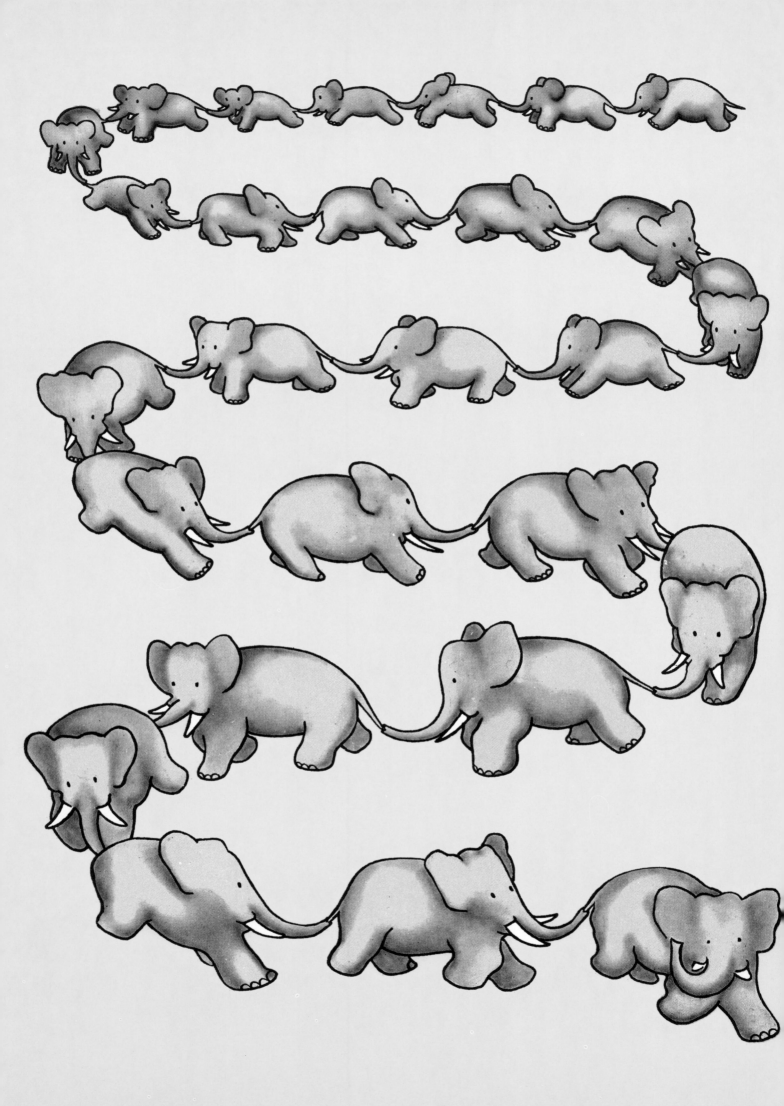

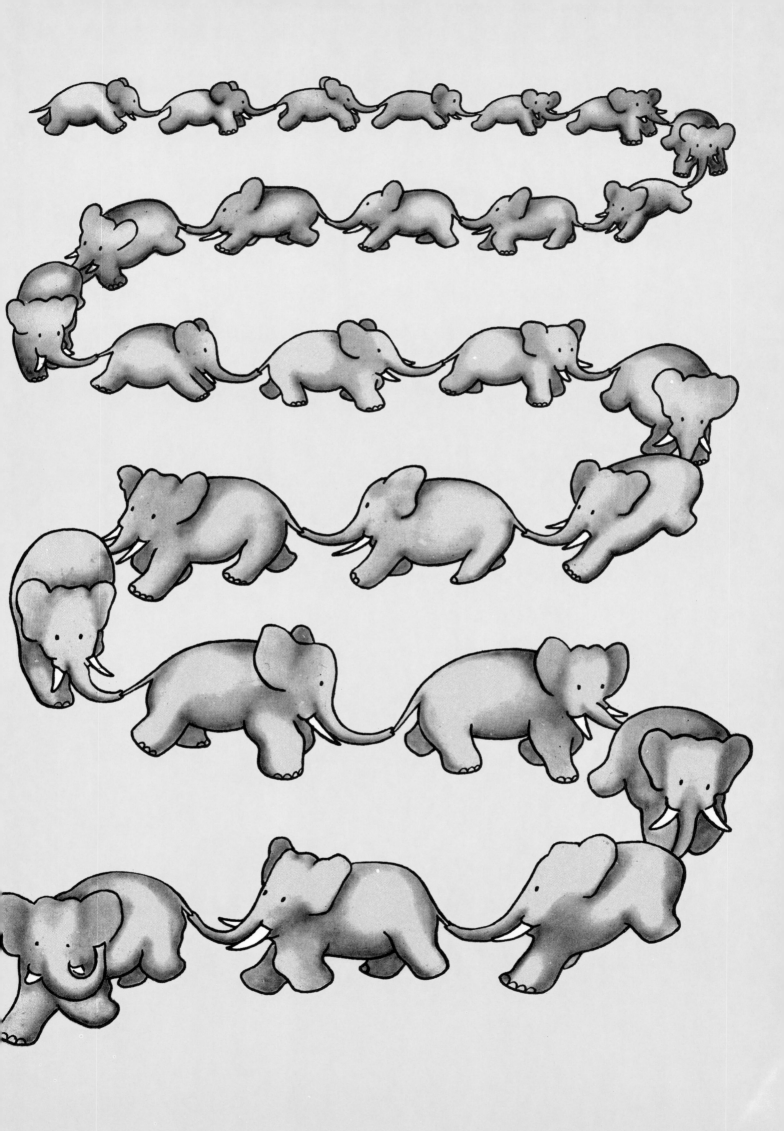